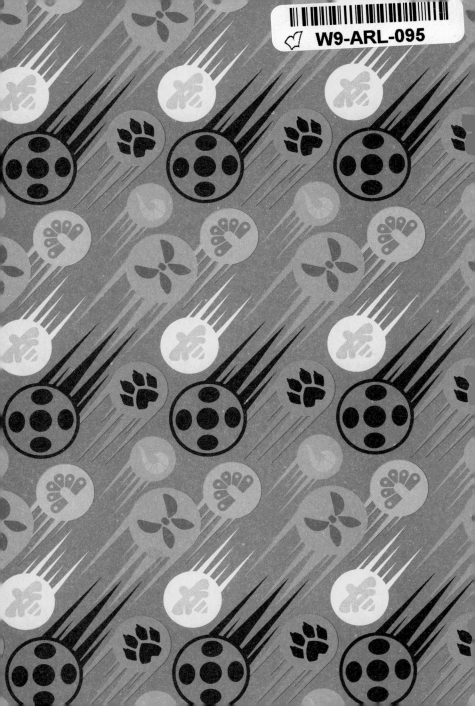

Peril in Paris

Miraculous™ is a trademark of ZAGTOON – Method.

Cover design by Sammy Yuen.

Little, Brown and Company
Hachette Book Group
1290 Avenue of the Americas, New York, NY 10104
Visit us at LBYR.com

Originally published in 2019 by Five Mile in Australia.
First U.S. Edition: September 2020

Little, Brown and Company is a division of Hachette Book Group, Inc. The Little, Brown name and logo are trademarks of Hachette Book Group, Inc.

The publisher is not responsible for websites (or their content) that are not owned by the publisher.

Library of Congress Control Number 2020905968

ISBNs: 978-0-316-42940-5 (pbk.), 978-0-316-42941-2 (ebook)

Printed in the United States of America

CW

10 9 8 7 6 5 4 3 2 1

Peril in Paris

L B

LITTLE, BROWN AND COMPANY
NEW YORK BOSTON

Marinette

Meet Marinette. She's a student, a babysitter, and a budding fashion designer. Marinette also has a pretty big secret that no one knows: When Paris is in trouble, she transforms into the superhero Ladybug!

This is Tikki →

Tikki is a mystical creature called a Kwami. She guides Marinette and helps her be the superhero Ladybug.

Marinette has a pair of earrings called the Ladybug Miraculous. They are magical. When Marinette needs to transform, she says, "Spots on!" and Tikki disappears into the earrings, turning Marinette into Ladybug.

Spots on!

Adrien

By day, Adrien is the perfect boy with the perfect life. But when Paris needs help, Adrien turns into Ladybug's superhero partner, Cat Noir.

This is Plagg →

Adrien's Kwami is called Plagg.

Plagg is generally lazy but can usually be convinced to help Cat Noir in return for some Camembert cheese.

Adrien's Miraculous is the Black Cat ring he wears on his right hand. When he needs to transform, Adrien says, "Claws out!" and Plagg disappears into his ring, turning Adrien into Cat Noir.

Claws out!

Hawk Moth

Hawk Moth is a master supervillain. He has the power to detect when someone is angry or sad. He harnesses that person's negative emtion and uses an akuma to transform them into a villain.

This is Nooroo ⟶

Nooroo is Hawk Moth's Kwami. He doesn't approve of how Hawk Moth uses his power, but he has no control over the villian.

Akumas are dark moths that infect people and create a mental connection between them and Hawk Moth. In return for the incredible evil powers Hawk Moth grants his victims, the akumatized are compelled to steal Ladybug's and Cat Noir's Miraculouses. Combined, these two Miraculouses would give Hawk Moth absolute power.

When Hawk Moth uses an akuma to infect Aurore Beauréal's umbrella, she is transformed into the weather-controlling villain, Stormy Weather.

With her weaponized umbrella, Stormy Weather can create any weather she likes, from snow and hailstorms to lightning and small hurricanes. By controlling the air and wind, Stormy Weather can also levitate and fly.

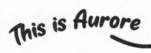

This is Aurore

Chapter 1

It's a perfect summer day in the 21st district of Paris! But instead of enjoying the sunshine, Marinette is in her apartment watching TV.

"Welcome to our Kidz+ Miss Weather finals," the host shouts into the camera. "Today, one lucky winner will be announced as our brand-new Kidz+ weather girl!"

The outcome of the Kidz+ Miss Weather competition has been all anyone at Marinette's school has talked about for weeks! Five thousand teenage girls auditioned to become the channel's new weather girl. After weeks of elimination rounds, there are only two finalists left: Aurore Beauréal and Mireille Caquet.

Marinette admires Aurore's style—she would make a great model for some of Marinette's designs. But Marinette hopes the sweet, humble Mireille will be the winner.

On television, the two girls are getting out of a limousine and walking down the red carpet toward the Kids+ TV studio. Marinette can't believe how calm they seem. She would be so nervous if millions of people were watching her on television. She would probably fall out of the limousine and faceplant on the red carpet!

Marinette's attention is pulled away from the television by a high-pitched giggle. She turns and gasps in horror. "Manon!"

A young girl, Manon, is charging around Marinette's apartment like a tornado. Even worse, she's wearing Marinette's latest creation on her head! It's a hat Marinette's been working on for days!

"Come on, Manon," Marinette pleads with the child while lunging at her. "Give that back!"

"But I want to be a fashion designer, too!" Manon shouts. She dodges Marinette, clutching the hat tightly to her tiny head.

Marinette suddenly feels bad. She has been so distracted by the Kidz+ finals that she almost forgot about today's important mission. No, it's not fighting alongside Cat Noir and saving Paris. Today's mission is one thousand times more dangerous. Marinette is babysitting a four-year-old for the afternoon!

Marinette is pretty fast (being a secret superhero

and all), but this kid is fast *and* sneaky! Manon leaps up onto the sofa, squealing with delight. Marinette launches herself across the room and dives straight into the cushions where Manon was just standing. *Oof!*

"Manon, please, it's not finished!" she shouts.

But Manon is too quick. She jumps off the couch and ducks under the sewing machine. Marinette follows, banging her head on the table. *Ouch! How can someone so small move so fast?* she wonders. *Maybe Manon is a superhero, too!*

"Oh! You're going to ruin it!" Marinette cries desperately. She loves her designs so much. One of Marinette's big dreams in life is to become a fashion designer. She loves sewing and creating, and she makes all her own clothes and accessories. Marinette gets such a buzz using her imagination and designing new pieces, just like the hat currently on Manon's head! *Oh no! Where is she?*

Manon seems to have vanished. Marinette crawls around the floor, looking under the couch. What is it with this kid?

Aha! Marinette spots a small Manon-shaped shadow near the window and smiles. *Imagine a four-year-old believing that she could outsmart a teenager who also happens to be the secret superhero Ladybug!* Marinette thinks. She tiptoes across the floor, slides along the wall, and pulls back the curtain in one swift movement! "Got you!" she cries triumphantly.

A doll wearing Marinette's hat stares back at her with glassy plastic eyes.

"I'm going to vote for Mireille! She's the best!" says a voice behind Marinette.

Marinette turns to see Manon in front of the television, tapping on Marinette's phone.

"Hey!" Marinette shouts. "My phone!" She grabs the phone. At the same time, Manon swipes the hat back and the chase is on again!

As Marinette runs down the hallway, she can't remember ever feeling this exhausted! Sure, Manon is a cutie, with her giant brown eyes and angel face, but Marinette would take a supervillain over a four-year-old any day. "Why did I agree to do this again?" she puffs.

Marinette hears a tinkling laugh from behind her and spins around. It's her Kwami, Tikki, hovering behind her.

"Stay low, Tikki," Marinette whispers, and she looks around anxiously. "Don't let Manon see you!"

Marinette knows Manon would love Tikki. Small enough to fit in Marinette's purse, Tikki is bright-red with a big, black spot on her forehead and violet eyes that sparkle. In other words, a four-year-old's dream playmate come true! Unfortunately,

Marinette can't let Manon spot her mystical companion.

Tikki is the sworn guardian of Marinette's superhero alter ego, Ladybug, and her magic powers allow Marinette to transform. Tikki has enjoyed watching over Marinette ever since the little Kwami first appeared in a burst of light and explained Marinette's new role as a superhero.

"Don't worry." Tikki laughs. "If you can handle Manon for a day, any villain here on out will be a piece of cake!"

The doorbell rings, and Tikki immediately ducks out of sight. Marinette fantasizes that the person at the door is someone to save her from this babysitting torment. Maybe it's a fairy who knows the spell for turning a small monster into a statue! At least for the afternoon. Marinette opens the door to find someone much better than a fairy.

"Alya!"

"Hey, I've got a huge scoop for you!" Alya says, entering the apartment.

Alya is Marinette's best friend, and she loves using words like *scoop*. Alya wants to be a news reporter, and she is always looking for a fresh story. Alya also runs the school blog. She is desperate to get an exclusive interview with Ladybug but has no idea that the superhero is actually her best friend!

"Guess who's on a photo shoot in the park?" Alya asks. Without even waiting for an answer, she holds out her phone. On the screen is a picture of Marinette's crush, Adrien, posing for a photographer.

Marinette's heart almost leaps out of her chest with excitement! If becoming a fashion designer is Marinette's first dream in life, then her second dream is to tell Adrien that she has been in love with him from the moment he entered her classroom. Not only is Adrien gorgeous, but he's also super smart. He speaks Chinese, is a champion fencer, and plays piano like Mozart. Unfortunately, there are two huge problems that are stopping Marinette from telling Adrien how she feels about him:

1. Every single girl at school—including the spoiled, beautiful, and rich Chloé Bourgois—is in love with him.

2. Whenever Marinette gets anywhere near Adrien, it's an epic *fail*! She turns as red as a tomato, her legs tremble, and it feels as if her mouth is suddenly full of cotton.

Marinette stares intently at Alya's phone and then at her friend. "*Now?!*" Marinette cries. "Adrien is in the park right *now?*"

"As we speak," says Alya, grinning. "Modeling Daddy Dearest's latest line."

Everyone in Paris knows Adrien's father is a famous designer and that Adrien models his clothes. Marinette also knows that Adrien only models to make his father happy. He doesn't enjoy posing for photos and would never brag or show off about it. It's just one of the many reasons Marinette adores him.

Marinette can't believe her luck. The park is right across the street from her apartment! She wonders if she can take a casual stroll through the park and "accidentally" bump into him. She's never had a chance like this at school, not with Chloé and the other girls always hanging around.

"Alya, this is brilliant! I can…" But Marinette

suddenly looks worried. "Hold on, what am I going to say to him?"

"The same thing as usual," Alysa teases. "'I... uh...ah...gah...ugh...'"

"Stop it," Marinette says, laughing along.

Alya knows better than anyone how hard Marinette finds it to speak once she's standing in front of Adrien.

"You wait!" Marinette says. "I *will* speak to him! And this time he'll actually understand what I'm saying. I swear it...on my sewing machine!"

"Who's she?" asks Alya.

A curious Manon is peeking up at Alya from between Marinette's legs.

"Oops," Marinette says. "Forgot about this little detail."

Alya smiles and bends down to inspect the tiny ball of energy hiding behind Marinette.

"This is Manon," Marinette explains. "One

of Mom's friend's daughters. I'm watching her all afternoon and—" She stops and gasps. "Oh no!" she cries. "I can't go out! I'm babysitting!"

"Let me guess," Alya says, rolling her eyes. "Another 'you couldn't say no' favor?"

"No! I…uh…I…uh…I…just…just"—Marinette hangs her head—"couldn't say no."

"No problem," Alya says. "I'll look after your little detail for you."

Marinette beams and turns to Manon, who instantly giggles and runs away. Marinette's hopes deflate like a popped balloon. It wouldn't be fair to leave a handful like Manon with Alya.

"Thanks, but I'm responsible for her. Besides, I couldn't do that to you. She's"—Marinette grits her teeth—"an absolute…angel."

Crash! Manon runs out of the kitchen. She waves a pan and a spatula above her head and zips madly around the room.

"Manon!" Marinette begins to chase her. "Give me those!" She manages to grab them out of Manon's hands before she can destroy the apartment.

"You're a total pushover, Marinette," Alya says, shaking her head. "I have to babysit my sisters all the time, which makes me an expert in dealing with 'angels.'"

Little Manon glares at Alya. "Who are you, anyway?"

"I'm a mythical unicorn from the world of Reespa!" Alya says, squatting down so she is at eye level with Manon. "Disguised as a totally fabulous human girl. I grant magical wishes, but only to little monkeys who behave!"

"No, you're not!" Manon laughs, then pauses and blinks. "Are you?"

Alya sweeps Manon up in her arms and throws her gently in the air. Manon squeals with delight.

"Okay," Alya says, plonking Manon down on Marinette's shoulders. "Let's all go to the park!"

"Yay!" Manon shouts, throwing her arms in the air. "Will you take me on the carousel, Marinette?"

"Sure!"

Marinette silently marvels at Alya's skills as they leave the apartment. Not only is Alya a soon-to-be world-famous reporter, but she's also an expert monkey wrangler! Marinette can't believe how lucky she is to have a best friend as clever as Alya.

More important, now she can see Adrien and hopefully make her dream come true!

Chapter 2

"This is the moment we've been waiting for! The viewers at home have made their decision!"

In the Kidz+ studio, the host stands between the two finalists, Aurore and Mireille, eager to announce the new Miss Weather. The audience leans forward, breathless with excitement.

The two girls have very different thoughts running through their heads. Aurore is already mentally preparing her acceptance speech. She has style, beauty, grace, and personality—everything it takes to be Miss Weather. Mireille is not as confident. She can't believe she's standing on the stage as a finalist. Although Mireille hopes there's a chance she'll be chosen, she is also ready to accept her loss and be happy for Aurore.

"The new Kidz+ weather girl is…"

Aurore opens her umbrella, which is perfectly accessorized to match her blue-and-white dress. She lifts her chin and beams her winner's smile into the cameras, waiting to hear her name.

"…Mireille!"

Aurore's jaw drops open in astonishment.

"Congratulations!" the host exclaims, turning to Mireille and shaking her limp hand.

Mireille is totally shocked. "Th-thank you," she eventually stammers.

Aurore's smile is gone, replaced with a look of fury.

"Mireille totally crushed you!" the host says to Aurore. "Better luck next time!"

Aurore glares at him and stomps off-set, leaving a still-dazed Mireille staring down the barrel of the camera.

"What's the big deal?" The host laughs as he watches Aurore storm her way off the studio stage. "You only lost by half a million votes!"

• • •

From within his secret lair, hidden high above Paris, the master supervillain, Hawk Moth, chuckles as he senses Aurore's fury.

"The vibrations are so strong." His deep voice echoes around the cavernous room. "I can feel the imminent anger and sadness! A moment of weakness from my next victim!"

Hawk Moth's ultimate goal is to steal Ladybug's and Cat Noir's Miraculouses. But to do so, he needs the energy of negative emotions. The moment Hawk Moth detects that someone is angry, bitter, or sad, he seizes the opportunity to use their emotions to his advantage.

And Aurore's rage is the perfect opportunity. The tall, sleek Hawk Moth clutches his thin black walking stick in his gloved hands. A silver mask covers his head, leaving only his eyes and evil grin visible. He closes his eyes as thousands of white butterflies flutter around him and a panel in the wall slides back to reveal a large, round window.

Hawk Moth opens his eyes and one of his hands. One of the butterflies flies down to land on his open palm.

"Such easy prey for my akuma!" he hisses, placing his other hand over the butterfly. Black spots fill his palm, and the butterfly transforms into a dark-purple moth with bright-white edges. It is identical in shape to the outline of the moth on Hawk Moth's mask.

Hawk Moth chuckles as the now-evil akuma flies out the window to search the city of Paris for Aurore Beauréal.

• • •

Aurore is shaking with rage. Ugly thoughts race through her brain as she jabs at the elevator button in the Kidz+ building.

The elevator arrives. As the doors close behind her, Aurore sinks to the floor. Now that she's alone she finally allows the angry stream of words to pour out of her mouth.

"I should have won!" she complains to the empty elevator. "I have the talent, the star looks... *everything*! But she took everything away from me. *They* took everything away from me!"

Suddenly, the lights flicker on and off. The elevator shakes violently before coming to a grinding halt. Aurore hears a fluttering noise and watches as a strange, dark moth wriggles its way through the crack between the elevator doors. She shrieks and opens her umbrella to shield herself from this unwanted intruder.

The akuma, enchanted so it can combine with any object, flies straight at the umbrella and disappears into it. The umbrella's blue-and-white tip immediately changes to a deep black. Then, a mysterious force takes hold of Aurore. She drops the umbrella to the ground and flops back against the elevator wall as Hawk Moth's deep voice echoes inside her mind.

"So correct, you are," the mysterious voice says. *"You should have won. Yes."*

Aurore lifts her chin with a stony expression. She stands up as the beginnings of a mask appear on her face.

"I should have won!" she repeats. "Yes!"

"Stormy Weather," continues the deep voice. *"I am Hawk Moth. I give you the power to seek revenge on them as* my *weather girl."*

Aurore listens intently to the instructions being relayed into her head by this unseen person.

"All you have to do is bring me the Miraculouses," Hawk Moth says. *"Can you do that?"*

"Yes," Aurore answers confidently.

"That's my weather girl," Hawk Moth says. *"Show the world who the best weather girl really is."*

The elevator dings as the doors open at the ground floor of the studio building. A villain leaves the elevator. She is no longer recognizable as the former Miss Weather finalist. Aurore's dress is now a dark purple, and her blonde hair is striped with black and purple. On her face, she wears a black mask shaped like a moth, and she wields a black-and-purple umbrella umbrella. Aurore is the supervillain Stormy Weather!

Chapter 3

Adrien, his bodyguard, and the photographer are standing near the fountain when Marinette, Alya, and Manon enter the park. The three girls duck behind a tree before peeking out to watch Adrien posing for the camera. The photographer shouts encouraging words at Adrien in an Italian accent.

"*Magnifico!*" the photographer says, snapping one perfect shot after another. "Super! Come on now, I want to see hunger in your eyes!"

Marinette isn't too sure what hungry eyes are

supposed to look like, but she definitely agrees that Adrien is *magnifico*! *There he is, walking along the ledge of the fountain with perfect grace and balance. Now he's passing his hand through those beautiful blond locks, and now he's running toward me shouting, "Marinette, I've been waiting for you..."* Marinette catches herself daydreaming and stops. *If only!*

"Come on," Marinette says. "We're going to stroll over there real cool as if we just happened to be passing by."

"Then what?" asks Alya.

"Then...," Marinette says, closing her eyes as she imagines the scene. "I'll invite him out for a smoothie at the end of the photo shoot. Then we'll get married and live happily ever after in a beautiful house, have two kids—no...three—

and a dog! Maybe a cat? Nah, forget the cat...a hamster! I *love* hamsters!"

Marinette opens her eyes to find Alya and Manon staring at her. "Sorry." Marinette shrugs. "Got a bit carried away."

"Yep," Alya says. "Let's just start with 'just happened to be passing by,' and see if we can get to that smoothie?"

"Good plan," Marinette agrees. "Let's go."

Marinette leads the way, and the three walk single file around the back of the fountain.

"Remember," Marinette says. "Cool...just be cool."

Alya smiles at her friend's attempt at a casual stroll. Marinette looks more like some kind of weird robot tiptoeing through a minefield. She couldn't look less cool if she tried. Alya also notices that the three of them are now directly in the background of the photographer's shot.

"Uh…we couldn't be more invisible," Alya says sarcastically, nudging Marinette.

"Okay," Marinette says, herding them back toward the tree. "Let's start over."

Hearing voices, Adrien looks over his shoulder and spots the three girls. Marinette freezes. A fake frozen smile spreads across her face as she locks eyes with Adrien. He smiles casually and waves at them before turning back to the photographer.

"Did you see that?" Marinette says as she waves back at Adrien. "He waved at me!"

"Yeah, I saw it, too," Alya says. "Pretty normal since we're in the same class."

Although Adrien isn't looking over at them anymore, Marinette continues to wave awkwardly. Alya reaches out and gently slaps Marinette's hand down, but Marinette is beyond caring about being embarrassed. Adrien smiled *and* waved at her! This has got to be the best day of her life!

• • •

Meanwhile, Mireille steps into the Kidz+ elevator, eager to get home and celebrate with her family. As the elevator doors close, she finally has a chance to reflect on the whirlwind of the past few hours. She still can't quite believe that she won. She, Mireille Caquet, will be presenting the weather on TV! Mireille is still lost in happy thoughts when the elevator door opens at the ground floor. She looks up to see a strange girl standing in the foyer. The girl is wearing a purple dress with a lightning bolt on it and is holding a large purple umbrella. Mireille feels a little afraid of the intense-looking girl.

"I am Stormy Weather," the girl with the striped hair and mask says. The voice sounds strangely familiar to Mireille. "The only weather girl who *always* gets the forecast right!"

"What? Who?" Mireille asks nervously.

"And unfortunately for you," Stormy Weather continues as an evil grin spreads across her face, "there's a freak icy front moving in *right now*!"

Stormy Weather points the tip of her dark umbrella at Mireille and, with a loud whoosh and crack, thousands of icy shards shoot toward her.

The shards join together, forming a thick wall of ice that traps Mireille inside the elevator.

Stormy Weather laughs with sheer delight as a terrified Mireille bangs her fists on the hard ice.

"Help!" Mireille cries. "Somebody get me out of here!"

Stormy Weather ignores her and heads toward the entrance. Hundreds of photographers and fans are waiting outside to greet their new Kidz+ weather girl.

"Mireille! Mireille!" The cheers fade out slowly and the fans' happy expressions change to confusion as Stormy Weather, not Mireille, walks out onto the red carpet. The villain sticks out her chin and holds up her hands triumphantly to the waiting crowd.

"Where's Mireille?" a confused fan asks.

Stormy Weather's head snaps around and looks at the man with an ice-cold glare.

"Ugh!" she groans before turning back to the

crowd with an evil smile. "For all of you who voted for Mireille, I'd advise you move indoors. It's going to get very blustery!"

The fans frown at one another in confusion. What can this girl mean? Why would they need to move indoors on this beautiful calm day?

"Oh wait," Stormy Weather continues, her eyes narrowing. "Too late!"

Stormy Weather raises her umbrella and sweeps it across the crowd, spraying them all with a strong blast of wind. People scream, clinging to railings and one another as the rush of air knocks them off their feet. The wind is so strong that it eventually blows them across the sidewalk and away down the street. Pleased with her work, Stormy Weather grins and flies away to wreak more havoc on the citizens of Paris.

Chapter 4

"**B**ravo! That's it! Smile! Smile! Smile!" Back in the park, the photographer's enthusiasm is still going strong, as is Marinette's. She could happily watch Adrien pose for the camera for hours on end.

Manon's interest, however, is fading very fast. Sitting at Marinette's feet, the little girl lets out a huge bored sigh. But then she spots a man selling balloons with Mireille's face on them.

"Marinette!" she squeals, standing up and

grabbing Marinette's arm. "I want a balloon with Mireille on it! Can I have one? Marinette?"

But Marinette is so distracted by Adrien that she doesn't even hear Manon.

"*Marinette!*" the little girl shouts.

Marinette jumps in surprise. The photographer whirls around and glares at the three girls.

"*Silencio!*" he cries.

Sensing trouble, Adrien's bodyguard takes a step toward the girls. Built like a fridge, the bodyguard is at least six feet tall and has all the warmth of an iceberg. Just looking at him sends shivers down Marinette's spine.

"Come on," Manon pleads, still tugging on Marinette's arm. "Please!"

"Let's go, small fry," Alya says. "I'll get you that balloon."

"No!" Manon insists stubbornly. "I wanna go with Marinette."

Marinette glances at the bodyguard and the photographer again. They are both glaring at her now, willing her to silence Manon.

"I'll deal with it," she says with a sigh. "I *am* her babysitter."

"But what about Adrien?" Alya whispers.

Of course Marinette would much rather stay and enjoy watching Adrien's photo shoot, but she made a promise to her mom. She walks over to the balloon man with Manon and hands him some money. He presents Manon with a Mireille balloon.

"Come on," Marinette says. "Let's go back now."

"I wanna go on the merry-go-round!" Manon cries. She makes a run for the carousel in the corner of the park.

"No, no, no!" Marinette chases Manon and grabs her hand. "I've got to get back to Adr—"

Marinette stops as Manon gazes up at her with wide eyes and a sad expression.

"You promised," Manon says tearfully. "You aren't going to break your promise, are you?"

"Oh, please, please, not the puppy dog eyes!" Marinette begs. "You know I can't say no to those!"

Manon widens her eyes even more and holds her breath. She knows it won't take much more to win over Marinette.

"Awww." Marinette's heart melts, and she knows she's lost the battle.

"Yay!" Manon squeals, dragging Marinette over toward the carousel. Marinette can't help grinning at Manon's excitement. At least she knows Adrien will be in the park for a while. *One quick ride on the carousel with Manon*, Marinette tells herself, *and then back to talk to Adrien before he finishes up.*

• • •

By the fountain, Adrien is wishing he'd finished up long ago! He hates modeling at the best of times, but today's shoot is too painful for words. *How many times can I smile and pose for the camera before I pass out from boredom?* he wonders, accidentally letting a loud yawn escape. The photographer scowls and lowers his camera.

"No, no, no!" he shouts. "The boy has eaten too much spaghetti! We need some more energy! More *romance*! We need...a *girl*!"

The photographer spots Alya sitting under a nearby tree eating an apple while she waits for Marinette and Manon to return.

"You!" the photographer shouts, running over to Alya. "I need an extra!"

"Who?" Alya asks, looking around. "Me?"

"*Si!*" the photographer cries triumphantly. "To pose with Mr. Adrien."

Alya beams. This is the perfect opportunity for Marinette. "You don't want me," she says, trying desperately to think of an excuse. "I...uh...think I'm having an allergic reaction to this apple!"

Alya sticks out her tongue, pretending it's expanding inside her mouth. "I thnow thus the therson thoo need!" she mumbles to the confused photographer. "Hold that thought!"

Alya sprints away and finds Marinette helping Manon up onto a unicorn at the carousel.

"They need an extra to pose with Adrien!" Alya pants excitedly.

"*What?!*" Marinette cries. "Seriously?"

"Is that boy your boyfriend?" Manon asks, stroking the unicorn's neck.

"What?" Marinette squeals. "No! I mean… yes…I mean…no?"

"Go on!" Alya says, giving Marinette a little push. "What are you waiting for?"

"But what about Manon?" Marinette asks, feeling guilty.

"You take care of Prince Charming," Alya replies. She jumps up onto the unicorn behind

Manon. "And I'll take care of Miss Unicorn here. You don't know how to control her anyway."

"No way," Manon cries, crossing her arms. "Marinette's my babysitter."

"Trust me," Alya says to Marinette.

Alya turns to Manon and holds her arm out in a salute. "Unicorns *unite*!" she cries. "Let's go to Reespa and find us some little kids and grant those wishes! *Yeehaw!*"

"*Yeehaw!*" Manon repeats. She is instantly caught up in the game and forgets all about Marinette.

Marinette grins and dashes back toward the fountain. Maybe she could suggest that their first pose be a scene from *Romeo and Juliet*! How perfect would that be?!

• • •

Flying high above Marinette's head, Stormy Weather comes face-to-face with a floating Mireille

37

balloon that slipped through a young fan's fingers. The sight of her opponent's smiling face is enough to bring on a fresh wave of rage.

Almost at the fountain, Marinette hears a frightened cry behind her. She stops and turns to see Stormy Weather hovering above the carousel. Marinette watches in horror as the villain raises her umbrella and points it at the park. She triggers a blizzard that whirls around the carousel, covering it in an enormous dome of ice…with Alya and Manon trapped inside!

"Run!" the balloon man shouts. Everyone in the park begins to flee, screaming in fright. Marinette knows she has to save Manon and Alya—and stop this villain from causing any more damage! Adrien will just have to wait. She looks around for the best hiding place to transform into Ladybug.

Most of the time, it's a great thrill and honor to be a superhero. Marinette loves defending Paris against evil and saving innocent people, even if she sometimes wonders why she was chosen out of everyone in the city. But there's also a downside: Marinette constantly has to lie to her friends, teachers, and parents about where she's been. It isn't easy to lead a double life, especially when she has to skip class or run away in the middle of a conversation...or miss out on performing a romantic scene in the park with Adrien!

Marinette ducks behind a tree and opens her purse.

"Time to transform, Tikki!" Marinette says as the Kwami jumps out of the bag. *"Spots on!"*

Tikki transforms herself into an energy stream that then flows into Marinette's plain-colored earrings. The earrings turn red and grow five black spots as Marinette's transformation into Ladybug begins. In a hazy cloud of stars and sparks, Marinette's body is covered in a red suit with black polka dots all over it. A red-and-black mask also appears, covering Marinette's eyes and protecting her true identity.

Now that Marinette's transformation into Ladybug is complete, she is ready to take on this new villain!

As Ladybug runs back toward the carousel, she wonders if her superhero partner, Cat Noir, is somewhere close by to give her a helping hand.

Chapter 5

*N*ear the park fountain, frightened parkgoers run past Adrien. They scream in terror as Stormy Weather continues her wave of icy destruction.

Adrien turns just in time to see Stormy Weather use her umbrella to blast an empty stroller out of her path. It soars through the air and lands upside down in a tall tree. Adrien jumps down from the fountain and sprints toward his bag. He needs his Kwami, Plagg, so he can transform. Plagg goes everywhere with Adrien, staying hidden until he receives the signal to transform Adrien into the superhero, Cat Noir. Like Marinette, no one knows about Adrien's secret superhero identity.

Adrien kneels down and opens his bag, only to find it empty. "Plagg?" Adrien says, looking around and shaking his head. *"Plagg!"*

"I'm not here," a muffled voice answers from somewhere nearby. "I'm sleeping."

Adrien sighs. He is used to Plagg and his lazy ways, and Adrien knows the only thing that will lure his pesky Kwami out is Camembert cheese!

Adrien pulls a hunk of cheese from his pocket and waves it in the air. Within seconds, the strong scent lures Plagg out of his hiding spot—the photographer's camera case. Plagg is the same size as Tikki, but is black with a long tail, pointy ears, and piercing green cat eyes. He is also much naughtier than Marinette's Kwami!

"Aaah!" Plagg cries, opening his mouth wide and

flying straight at the cheese to take a bite.

Adrien pulls the cheese away from Plagg's open mouth and arches an eyebrow at the sassy Kwami.

"For your information," Plagg says, "I can smell Camembert in my sleep. It's only one of my *many* talents!"

"Great," Adrien says, dropping the cheese to the ground. "But there's no time to talk cheese. Plagg, *claws out!*"

Plagg groans. The cheese will have to wait. Adrien thrusts his fist into the air, and Plagg transforms into an energy stream. He flows into the Black Cat Miraculous ring on Adrien's finger and begins transforming Adrien into Cat Noir! Adrien's stylish outfit is replaced by a tight black suit, cat ears, and a mask. As Cat Noir, he brandishes a black staff, which he can use as a weapon or as a pole to vault along rooftops. Now

he is ready to take on Stormy
Weather alongside Ladybug. As
Cat Noir, not even the fiercest
tornado can frighten him!

• • •

Ladybug makes her way
back across the park, desperate
to get to Alya and Manon.

"Why did I leave Manon?"
she wonders out loud. "I
should have never done
that!"

Ladybug arrives at
the ice dome that covers
the carousel. She can see
Alya comforting Manon. The
little girl is trembling with cold and fear, and she
snuggles into Alya's arms. Ladybug's heart twists,
even though she knows Manon is in safe hands.

"I'll get you out of there!" she calls to Alya through the thick layer of ice.

Not even Marinette's best friend knows Ladybug's true identity, but Alya trusts the superhero to do everything she can to get her and Manon out of this situation.

"Let's wire-cut this icy cake!" Ladybug cries, launching her magical yo-yo at the thick dome.

The yo-yo rises in the air and wraps itself around the dome. Ladybug pulls tightly to slice the ice in half, but the dome is so slippery that the thread slides off! The yo-yo springs back up into the air and lands with a thud on top of Ladybug's head, knocking her to the ground.

"Or not," Ladybug says, getting back to her feet. "On to Plan B!"

Ladybug presses her hands against the ice wall to reassure Alya and Manon, who are now looking even more scared.

"Don't worry," she says calmly. "Everything's going to be okay."

"Where's Marinette?" Manon asks, staring up at Ladybug through the thick wall of ice.

"She hasn't forgotten about you, Manon," Ladybug says, squatting down so she is face-to-face with the tiny girl.

"How did you know my name?" Manon asks.

"Uh…um…Marinette told me." Ladybug can't believe she almost blew her cover! "She's coming right back, okay?"

Manon nods and places her hand against the ice so that it lines up with Ladybug's, and Alya gives the superhero the thumbs up. *Manon's being so brave*, Ladybug thinks. She doesn't want to leave them but knows she must.

• • •

Stormy Weather walks out of the park, still shooting icy blasts out of her umbrella.

"Hey, Ice Queen!"

Stormy Weather stops and looks up to see Cat Noir perched on top of the park fence.

"What's with all the terrorizing?" he asks. "Why don't you go pick on someone your own temperature?"

"My name is *not* Ice Queen," she snarls at him. "It's Stormy Weather!"

Cat Noir grins and hops down from the fence with ease. He swings his tail in lazy circles.

"Listen," he teases. "I'm *feline* more generous than usual today. So cool down and we'll call it quits, okay?"

Stormy Weather is in no mood for jokes. Before Cat Noir knows what's happening, he's blasted with a gust of wind that propels him into the sky. He soars over the tops of buildings and away from the park. Cat Noir eventually plummets back toward the ground, pinging between cars like a pinball before landing with a thud in the middle of the cobblestone road. Unfortunately for him, this is the moment Ladybug appears beside him.

"I thought cats always landed on their feet," she teases, holding out a hand to help the super-embarrassed superhero.

Ladybug and Cat Noir haven't known each other for very long, but their natural banter makes it seem as if they've been a superhero team forever. Ladybug thinks Cat Noir is kind of arrogant (and that his jokes are pretty terrible), but she knows she can always count on him whenever she needs him. Without his help, it would be a lot harder to defeat villains, so Ladybug puts up with the bad jokes. She has no idea that Cat Noir has a huge crush on her, and that right now he's feeling pretty ridiculous, lying in the middle of the road before her.

"Why, thanks, m'Ladybug," he says, trying to hide his embarrassment with a silly voice. "But I had it covered."

Keeping up the gentleman's role, Cat Noir leans down and kisses Ladybug's hand.

Ladybug pushes him away. "No time for your childish charm, Cat Noir, but you're welcome."

Stormy Weather swoops down and lands on the road nearby.

"We should be expecting lightning storms...,"
she says to the superhero team, an evil smile on
her face. "Like, right *now*!"

Lightning sparks appear from her umbrella.
The sky darkens and thunder rumbles. Then, a
huge bolt of lightning strikes directly at Cat Noir.
Ladybug pushes him out of the way just
in time, and the two roll along the road as

the lightning strikes the cobblestones behind them. The danger avoided, Cat Noir grins up at Ladybug. He's in the arms of the girl he adores and couldn't be more thrilled. Ladybug is not so thrilled. There's only one boy her heart beats for, and it certainly isn't the self-assured Cat Noir! She grabs his smug face and turns it toward Stormy Weather, who hovers over the road, furious at having her destructive plan foiled.

"You've just won yourself a cat fight!" Cat Noir declares, jumping to his feet and rushing toward Stormy Weather.

"*Black ice!*" the villain shouts, sending a full-blown blizzard toward him. The shards of ice connect to form a slippery surface on the road. Ladybug watches helplessly as the street turns into an ice rink beneath their feet.

Cat Noir slips and slides backward. Ladybug also finds herself sliding along the icy ground, powerless to fight back against such a strong wind. Cars lift from their parking spots and fly past the superheroes as they desperately reach out for something to grasp on to. Finally, Ladybug manages to lasso her yo-yo around a streetlight and anchor herself to it. She grabs Cat Noir by his tail as he flies past her.

"Gotcha!" she cries.

They cling to the pole, their feet dangling out behind them like flags flapping on a flagpole. Ladybug is wondering just how much longer she can hold on when the wind stops, and they fall heavily to the ground.

Stormy Weather advances toward them through the air, wreaking even more destruction on cars and buildings as she glides along. The sky is as black as soot, and smashed vehicles lie upside down all along the street. The villain pauses beside a large billboard that has Mireille's face on it and destroys it with a single blast. Ladybug can no longer recognize her beloved city; Stormy Weather seems determined to leave Paris in complete ruin. Ladybug must stop this villain and save Alya and Manon before they freeze. But how?

Cat Noir leaps up, dusting himself off and striking a cool superhero pose—a difficult thing to do after being blown along the street like a plastic bag! "A little Cat Noir will take the wind out of her sails!"

But Ladybug grabs his tail before he can take a step and pulls him back with a jolt. "Whoa, kitty-kitty!" Ladybug has had enough of his impulsive behavior. "You better think before you leap."

She lets go of him, and Cat Noir falls face-first onto the cobblestones before springing back to his feet again.

"You got a plan?" he asks.

"Just follow my lead." Ladybug sprints away and up the side of a nearby storefront, hopping from building to building. Cat Noir quickly catches on and leaps up onto the building on the opposite side of the street. The two superheroes run parallel along the sides of stores and office buildings, easily catching up to Stormy Weather and taking her by surprise.

The villain looks around to see Ladybug descending on her from one side, brandishing her yo-yo, and Cat Noir from the other side, spinning his staff.

"Not you again!" Stormy Weather raises her umbrella and blasts them both with another icy gust, blowing them up and along the tops of buildings, across treetops, and through the city. When they finally crash to the ground, they look up to see an avalanche of flying cars following in their wake.

"Look out!" Ladybug shouts.

Ladybug and Cat Noir use their acrobatic skills to avoid getting squashed by the cars raining down upon them. Just when they think there can't possibly be any left, a large bus plummets toward the ground, heading right for them!

Ladybug grabs Cat Noir, launching her yo-yo above their heads. The speed of it creates a force field above them. The bus drops down on top of them, but the force field slices a large hole in the metal wall. A moment later the heroes find themselves standing, unhurt, inside the upturned bus. Ladybug stops spinning the yo-yo, and it falls through the hole and into the bus, clonking Cat Noir on the head.

"*Ow!*" he cries.

Ladybug can't help giggling at the dazed expression on Cat Noir's face.

• • •

Meanwhile, firefighters use pickaxes to chip away at the icy dome surrounding the carousel. While they work, Alya sings and plays clapping games with Manon to try to distract her from their situation.

"Lemonade, crunchy ice," Alya sings. "Hit it once, hit it twice...*freeze!*" She leans back with her hands up and Manon falls forward, missing Alya's hands.

"Hey, no fair!" Manon complains. "You always win!"

There is a loud cracking noise over their heads.

"What was that?" Manon asks in a small voice.

Alya looks up and notices large pointy icicles beginning to push their way through the dome. She wonders how long they have before those sharp points reach them but is determined not to show Manon how worried she is.

"It's...uh...the big goblin king!" she says,

thinking quickly and adopting a deep voice. "He ate too much and split his shirt! *Aha-ha!*"

Alya chases a giggling Manon inside the icy dome until their game is interrupted by another loud cracking sound. Alya and Manon look up to see the icicles getting closer and closer.

Manon whimpers in fright.

"You...uh, wanna hear a story?" Alya asks. She grabs Manon and guides her under the carousel roof and away from the scary-looking icicles.

• • •

Now that she's managed to get rid of those annoying superheroes, Stormy Weather swoops down to land on a rooftop. She stops and listens as Hawk Moth's deep voice speaks to her through the enchanted akuma.

"You've shown them all who the real winner is, my weather girl," he says. *"But now is the time for you to fulfill your part of the agreement, and here's my plan...."*

Stormy Weather smiles as Hawk Moth relays his instructions to her.

• • •

"Maybe she's got some unresolved anger issues," Ladybug muses as she and Cat Noir run along the dark deserted streets of Paris.

"Or she didn't pass her driving test?" Cat Noir responds, looking at the destroyed cars littered around them.

"Hello, viewers!"

Ladybug and Cat Noir skid to a halt as they hear Stormy Weather's voice. They turn to see her face projected on a large screen in the street. There, the superheroes can see that Stormy Weather is broadcasting from the Kidz+ TV studio.

"Here's the latest forecast for the first day of summer," Stormy Weather announces, gesturing at a map of Paris with the tip of her umbrella. "Looks like Mother Nature had a change in plans. Summer vacation is officially *over*!"

"Already?" Cat Noir jokes. "But I look so good in a swimsuit!"

He glances at Ladybug, waiting for her to laugh. Ladybug is a little amused, but she would never show it. It would only make Cat Noir even smugger than he already is. Besides, she's in no mood for jokes. Snowflakes are already starting to fall, and if they don't stop Stormy Weather soon, the whole climate will be out of whack and could destroy Paris forever.

"The cat suit will do, thanks," Ladybug tells her partner. "At least now we know where to find her!"

Ladybug and Cat Noir head straight for the Kidz+ building. In the foyer, Stormy Weather's face fills every screen.

"Prepare for the worst weather in history," the villain sneers.

A large cardboard cutout of Aurore Beauréal stands in the foyer near one of the screens.

"That girl reminds me of someone!" Cat Noir says, pointing to the cutout.

"It's her!" Ladybug says, recognizing Aurore. "Stormy Weather! The akuma must be in her umbrella! Come on, she's broadcasting from the studio!"

They race up to the studio, but the door is locked. Together, Ladybug and Cat Noir kick it open and rush inside. The studio is empty.

"In Stormy Weather's world, it is a winter wonderland," they hear Stormy Weather say. *"Forever!"*

A television screen projecting the villain's forecast is sitting in the corner of the studio, a camera set up in front of it.

"It's a recording!" Ladybug says.

They hear an evil laugh and turn to see Stormy Weather standing in the doorway. She raises her umbrella and a bolt of lightning strikes the large, heavy lights on the studio ceiling. Ladybug and Cat Noir dive out of the way just as the lights fall. The lights crash to the ground, narrowly missing the superheroes.

The rest of the studio lights go out, plunging the room into darkness. Stormy Weather stops

and listens as Hawk Moth speaks to her again.

"This is all going wonderfully according to plan!" he says gleefully. *"Soon their Miraculouses will be mine! Bring them to me!"*

Stormy Weather nods and turns to run down the blacked-out hallway.

"Frosty the Snowgirl's getting away!" Cat Noir says, his cat eyes enabling him to see in the dark.

Unfortunately, Ladybug doesn't have the same power. She stands up, reaches her hands out in front of her, and moves to walk forward. The superhero takes only a few steps before she trips over the fallen lights on the ground.

"Do I hear a damsel in distress?" Cat Noir teases.

"Some of us don't have night vision!" Ladybug replies grumpily.

"No need to bug out," Cat Noir says, reaching 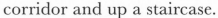 for her hand. "Just trust me!"

"Whoa!" Ladybug cries as Cat Noir pulls her to her feet and drags her through the dark corridor and up a staircase.

Chapter 6

Alya is running out of stories to keep Manon distracted while the firefighters continue chipping away at the ice without any luck.

"And as soon as she took a bite of the cursed potato," Alya says, Manon snuggled on her lap, "the poor princess fell into a deep, deep sleep."

A large icicle pushes its way through the roof of the carousel, making them both gasp.

"Hurry up, Ladybug," Alya mumbles quietly, and she holds Manon closer to her chest.

Ladybug can hear Stormy Weather laughing as Cat Noir drags his partner behind him up flight after flight of stairs in the pitch darkness.

"Okay, that's enough," Ladybug pants. "I think I can manage to—"

"*Duck!*" Cat Noir cries.

Ladybug ducks and hears a heavy object whiz past her head and clatter down the stairs behind her. Stormy Weather is throwing things down the staircase at them!

"Follow your lead on this one!" Ladybug finishes. She hates to admit it, but she needs Cat Noir. She can't see a thing, and he's their only hope for stopping Stormy Weather.

Finally, Cat Noir pushes a door open, and they find themselves out on the snowy and brightly lit rooftop. As her eyes adjust to the light, Ladybug spots Stormy Weather hovering in the sky above them.

"You airheads!" the villain chuckles. "You fell right into my trap!"

Stormy Weather opens up her umbrella and conjures a powerful whirlwind that slowly circles them on the rooftop. It grows in strength and speed until the whole building is surrounded by a swirling tornado.

"*The time is now!*" Hawk Moth tells Stormy Weather. "*Bring me the Miraculouses!*"

"There's no way out," Stormy Weather shouts down to the superheroes. "Party's over, fools!"

Ladybug takes a step toward the villain. "We're just—"

She stops and looks down. Cat Noir is still holding on to her hand. Noticing Ladybug's expression, he gives an embarrassed chuckle and releases her.

"We're just getting started, Stormy!" Ladybug cries. *"Lucky Charm!"* Ladybug throws her yo-yo up in the air, knowing that her Lucky Charm power is her final chance to stop Stormy Weather.

As Ladybug releases the yo-yo, a swarm of ladybugs fly out. Ladybug waits for them to turn into a mystery object, which she must then use to stop the villain. The superhero knows that once she has used this power, her earrings will begin to flash, and the five black spots will disappear one by one. Once five minutes are up and all the black spots have faded, Ladybug will transform back into Marinette. This is the part of being a superhero where she must use her brain as well as her strength!

Ladybug and Cat Noir blink in astonishment as a red towel with black spots falls into Ladybug's arms.

"A bath towel?" Ladybug says, looking very confused. "What am I supposed to do with this?"

"Great!" Cat Noir scoffs. "So, we're about to be obliterated, but at least we'll be dry!"

"Just hold your whiskers!" Ladybug says. She wraps the towel around her arm while she thinks about how to use it.

"Hail!" Stormy Weather commands, lifting her umbrella back to the skies.

A shower of hailstones as big as ping-pong balls

begin to fall on Cat Noir and Ladybug. Cat Noir pulls out his stick and spins it over their heads to deflect the hail.

"So, what's the plan for getting the akuma back?" he shouts to Ladybug over the noise of the hailstorm. "My arm's starting to get a cramp!"

Ladybug's super senses activate, and she surveys every element on the rooftop around them: a pipe, a large panel, a railing. She glances down at the towel around her arm.

Aha! She's got it!

"See that sign over there?" Ladybug calls to Cat Noir. She points to the back of the large billboard. "Check it out!"

Cat Noir nods in understanding and springs into action. *"Cataclysm!"* he cries, holding out his hand and summoning his own special power. A cloud of black particles form in his palm, charging it with magical energy. Cat Noir now has the power to destroy anything he touches, a useful skill for slowing down a supervillain! Like Ladybug's power, Cataclysm prompts a countdown on Cat Noir's ring that will transform him back into Adrien. He starts running toward the sign.

"Hey, *Cold*ilocks!" he taunts. "Is that all you got?"

An infuriated Stormy Weather stops the hail and calls bolts of lightning to rain down on him instead. Cat Noir must jump, leap, and spin just like a nimble cat to avoid the lightning as it strikes the rooftop.

Cat Noir finally makes it to the billboard and runs his sharpened claws along the bottom of it. The rails holding it in place buckle and bend, and the sign begins to collapse, falling straight into Stormy Weather's path. She ducks out of the way just in time, but the distraction is all Ladybug needs to complete her plan.

Ladybug throws her yo-yo up in the air, and the string wraps itself around Stormy Weather's ankle. Holding firmly to the thread, Ladybug runs under a pipe and jumps over a large ventilation fan, causing the arm of a crane to rotate. Now is

the moment to use the tool Lucky Charm gave her!

Ladybug holds the towel over her head, creating a parachute. The towel swells from the flow of air, lifting Ladybug up into the sky. As she rises, Stormy Weather, still connected to Ladybug by the yo-yo, begins to descend. Just as Ladybug had planned, Stormy Weather descends quickly, and the rotating arm knocks the umbrella out of her hand. Cat Noir leaps nimbly to catch it.

Cat Noir throws the umbrella to Ladybug as she lands back on the roof. With one swift action, Ladybug breaks the umbrella in two across her knee, and the offending akuma flies out!

"Get out of here, you nasty bug," Ladybug says, throwing the umbrella onto the rooftop. "No more evildoing for you."

Ladybug opens her yo-yo and spins it toward the escaping akuma. "Time to de-evilize!" she cries as the yo-yo closes around the akuma. The lid snaps shut, trapping it inside. "Gotcha!"

Ladybug opens the yo-yo and the akuma, now transformed back into a beautiful white butterfly, flutters away

"Bye-bye, little butterfly," says Ladybug.

Ladybug tosses the towel high in the sky above Paris and shouts, "Miraculous Ladybug!"

The towel transforms into an army of magic ladybugs. The ladybugs zoom across the city, repairing streets, buildings, cars, and anything else that has been damaged by Stormy Weather.

Finally, the clouds clear, the sun shines, and Stormy Weather transforms back into a very dazed Aurore Beauréal.

"Huh?" Aurore murmurs, confused to find herself lying on top of a building. "What am I doing up here?"

Back in Hawk Moth's secret lair, the master supervillian is furious. He has been foiled by Ladybug and Cat Noir again!

"Someday," he vows, "your Miraculouses will be all mine! I don't care how many enemies I need to throw at you to win, but I will be *victorious!*"

Oblivious to Hawk Moth's sinister threat, Ladybug and Cat Noir fist-bump each other on the roof.

"*Pound it!*" they cheer.

Ladybug grins as Cat Noir leaps off the rooftop

and out of sight. Even if he is a little annoying, they make a great team…but he's still no Adrien.

"Oh no!" Ladybug cries. "Adrien! Alya and Manon!"

• • •

Marinette and Tikki arrive back in the park to find Alya and Manon standing beside the carousel, with no icy dome in sight! Marinette waves, relieved to see them safe.

"Hey," says Tikki, poking out from Marinette's purse. "There's Adrien and the photographer waiting for you!"

"You don't think it's too late?"

"Come on, Marinette," Tikki says. "You saved Manon *and* the whole world today! Have some fun!"

Marinette laughs, then turns around as she hears a voice call her name.

"Marinette!" Manon leaps into Marinette's arms and Marinette squeezes her tightly.

"Oh, Manon!" she cries.

"I know what your secret is!" Manon says in a singsong voice.

Marinette freezes. "Wha-what secret?" she asks nervously. What will she do now that Manon knows the truth about who she really is?

"Ladybug is your best friend!" Manon says with a grin. "That's how you both always know what the other one's going to do!"

Marinette breathes a sigh of relief and gives Manon another squeeze.

"Wait!"

The three girls turn to see the photographer from Adrien's photo shoot watching them with a rapturous look on his face.

"Who is that angel?" he asks, pointing at Manon. "I must have her in my photo shoot!"

Only a few minutes later, Marinette and Alya stand back and watch Manon pose with Adrien. Marinette can't believe it is Manon and not her who is in Adrien's arms, holding his hand and kissing his cheek.

Alya puts her arm around her best friend and pats her back sympathetically.

Marinette can't help laughing. *Oh well,* she thinks as Manon turns to blow her a kiss, *at least I won someone's heart today…even if it wasn't the one I expected!*

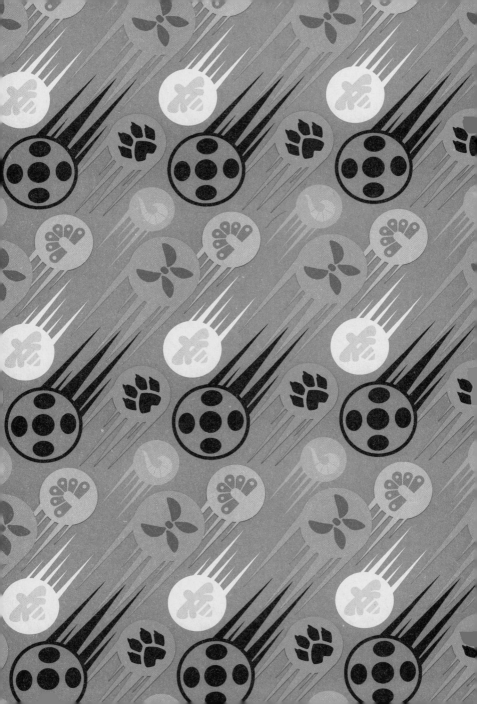

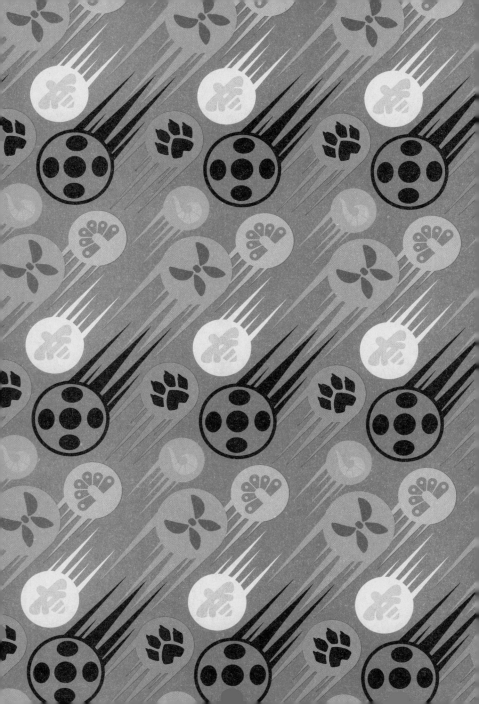